Thank you for being my teacher.

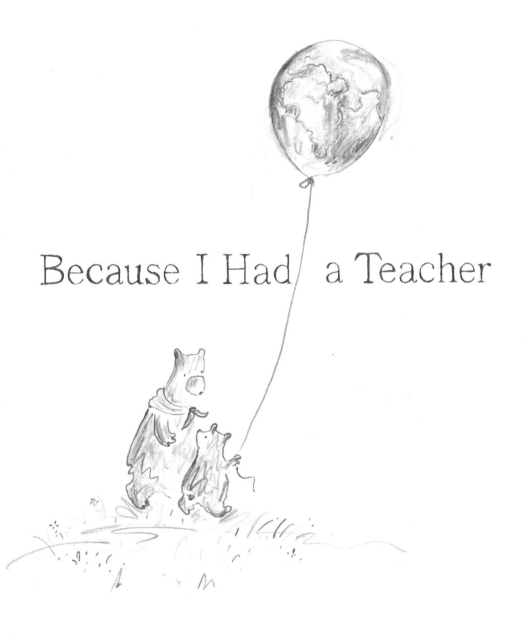

Because I Had a Teacher

Written by Kobi Yamada   Illustrated by Natalie Russell

Because I had a teacher,
I love to learn.

I discovered that I can do much
more than I thought I could.

I realized it's okay when some
things are harder than others.

I found that challenges can be fun.

Because I had a teacher,
I discovered that there are
lots of ways of being smart.

And I know that mistakes are
just part of getting something right.

I realized that some of the
hardest things for me to do
make me feel the proudest.

Because I had a teacher,
I know how good it feels when
someone is happy to see me.

I know that I can always ask for help.

I feel like I have a friend on my side.

I see that some of the most important
things are said without words.

Because I had a teacher,
I have whole new worlds to explore.

I discovered that what I can
imagine, I can make real.

And now I feel like I can do anything.

Because I had you,
I learned to believe in me.

COMPENDIUM.
live inspired

Thank you to Mr. Gotchy. A truly extraordinary teacher. ~K.Y.

To Maxine—an amazing teacher! ~N.R.

With special thanks to the entire Compendium
family and to teachers everywhere.

CREDITS:

Written by: Kobi Yamada

Illustrated by: Natalie Russell

Designed by: Sarah Forster

Edited by: Amelia Riedler, M.H. Clark & Ruth Austin

Library of Congress Control Number: 2016945645
ISBN: 978-1-943200-08-5

2nd printing. Printed in China with soy inks. A031701002